W9-CDV-785

WITHDRAWN
BY
WILLIAMSBURG REGIONAL LIBRARY

One morning, in a very old city filled with boats, people, prayers, and hot tea, a man hands you a flapping fish.

You say thank you and hold the fish tight, but it is gasping for water,

so you throw it back into the sea.
You're afraid the fisherman
will be angry.

Instead, he pats you on the head and waves to his friend the simit seller.

The simit seller hands you one of her sesame rounds. You thank her and take a bite, and the bread is still crunchy and warm.

Soon, you're surrounded by seagulls. You break off a piece and throw it into the air, and the gulls take turns diving until your bread is all gone.

The simit seller understands. Her eyes twinkle as she whistles across the street to the ferry captain, who welcomes you with a smile.

From the boat, the city whispers something you don't quite understand. The water shines for you. The freight ships sing low. Dozens of jellyfish dance in the depths.

After three bridges and one palace, you start to shiver, so a man with wobbly legs hands you a steaming-hot tea. You thank him, drop a sugar cube in, and stir the drink with a silver spoon.

A boy with an accordion plays a song that slows down the ships and quiets the dolphins. Around you, the other passengers close their eyes, humming the music.

When he's finished, the boy takes a bow and holds out his hand. Some people give him a coin, but you don't have any, so you hand him the silver spoon. The wobbly man winks at you.

The boy takes your hand and you run off the boat together,

past the captain, across the Galata Bridge,

to the entrance of the Spice Bazaar.

Everywhere you turn, someone hands you something—a walnut, a bunch of olives, dozens of candies that taste like roses and stick to your teeth.

When your pockets are full, the boy leads you to a secret rooftop, and you sit there eating and watching the boats go from one sea to another.

You give him your last rose candy,

and he tells you the story of the boy and the girl in the lonely tower in the middle of the sea. You think maybe he knows what the city was whispering.

But before you can ask, the boy is up

and running fast toward the Grand Bazaar.

You run after him and look everywhere, behind carpets and lanterns and strands of gold, but the boy is gone, and you are thirsty and lost and a little bit tired.

Across the street, a man is selling pomegranate juice.

With nothing left to give him, you share the story of your day, from the fish to the boat to the accordion boy.

The man splits the fruit and hands you the juice.

As you drink it, a tiny kitten rubs against your legs, trembling and meowing.

You take the straw out of your juice and feed the kitten, until it's all finished. The juice man strokes the kitten and calls over to his wife, who kisses the top of your head . . .

and leads you into
a hot room made
of marble.

She wraps you in a towel,
ties a knot around your waist,
and takes you to a tub,

where she scrubs you
until the whole day is
gone and there is only
you and the water.

After that, she covers you in a blanket of bubbles, which makes you giggle and the wife giggle and her friend giggle and so on, until all the women around you are clean and giggling.

When you are dry, you put on your old clothes and walk outside

just as the sun is going down
and hitting the rooftops.

The tiles look like the scales of a fish.

A song comes out of the sky.

It sounds like a gift.

So you say thank you, hold it, and let it go.